Panda Myths

by Hong Kong Kids

Edited by Judy J. Butler

History of the Panda Myth Project

by Judy Butler

In the summer of 2007, my students and I began to watch the live coverage of Hong Kong's four pandas on television. I read them many stories about pandas; we looked at video clips on You Tube of Hong Kong's pandas and pandas around the world. The students wrote poems about pandas. In the spring, I thought it would be fantastic for each student to pick a characteristic of the panda and write a myth (a fictional story that explains something in nature) to tell how the panda came to look like it does today. It was a lengthy project with many rewrites. Each student took home a "published" copy with a dedication, panda myth, illustrations and author's note with a photograph. Their spiral bound books looked fabulous. I thought, "Wouldn't it be great to get their stories printed in a small book and sell them in Hong Kong and give all proceeds to WWF for conservation of pandas!" As the students were working on their stories, the big earthquake in Sichuan occurred. Because many of the pandas' habitats were damaged, it seemed like the panda project came at a perfect time. Here are nineteen unique stories explaining why pandas look the way they do today.

The Myths

NOW...

Why Pandas Have Eye Patches

Veronica Ahn

To my mom and my dad

Long, long ago, pandas had no eye patches. They only had black ears, black legs, black noses, black chests and black stripes across their backs.

One day pandas and rabbits had a competition to see who could play the best joke. The pandas played an amazing joke on the rabbits that made the rabbits get so mad!

One day a rabbit found a pair of binoculars hanging on a tree. The rabbit thought of a perfect plan. That day, when everyone was asleep, she took the binoculars out and outlined the rims with black permanent ink. Then she walked outside silently and she hung the binoculars back on the tree.

The next day, the rabbit brought a panda on a picnic near the tree. "Look!" said the rabbit, "What is that?"

"I don't know! I want to try it on," said the panda as he reached out for the binoculars. As the panda started to reach the binoculars, the rabbit started grinning. "Everything is so big!" shouted the panda with wonder, "I'll bring this home to show my parents!" The rabbit tried not to laugh.

When they went to a lake to drink water, the panda saw what had happened to his eyes. He had big, black eye patches! The panda got so angry and very upset with the rabbit. He tried to wash the ink off, but he couldn't. It was permanent ink.

From that day until now, pandas have big, black eye patches.

Veronica Ahn
was born in Korea in 1996. She has lived in many different parts of the world, including Australia, Germany and now Hong Kong. She is going to year 7 at German Swiss International School. She loves to read, watch movies and hang out with her friends. She also likes to travel around the world.

BEFORE

NOW...

Why Pandas Have Black Eye Patches

Rachel Chang

With special thanks to my mom, Harris Shuen
and to my best friend, Natalie

Many, many years ago, all pandas had small dark brown eyes, but the fur around their eyes was white.

The pandas lived in the mountains in China. They liked to draw pictures in their free time. One day the pandas drew pictures of themselves on many bamboo stalks in the bamboo forest. They used black ink to draw. One panda used white ink to draw. Most of the pandas liked black ink. They didn't want the panda to use white ink.

They all said to that panda, "You have to use black ink." It didn't listen to the other pandas. So the other pandas put the black ink on its face. They used a brush to paint circles around its eyes.

So, that is why pandas have black eye patches.

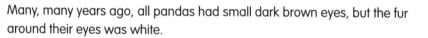

Rachel Chang

is seven years old. She learns in Sacred Heart Canossian Primary School. Her hobbies are drawing and singing. She likes to eat fruit, potato chips and French fries. She likes dolls; her favorite doll is Kuromi. She likes to swing at the playground.

BEFORE...

NOW

Why Pandas Move So Slowly

Karissa Cheung

For my parents and my best friend Ally,
who loves pandas

Many years ago, all pandas ran so fast! They could run as fast as monkeys when they climbed the bamboo trees. They liked to eat, too, but they were not very fat because they always exercised.

One day, two pandas played together. When they were chasing after each other, one panda tripped over a stone and then both of them fell down and they injured their legs.

They rested for three weeks. While they were resting, they felt bored. They loved to eat bamboo, so they crunched and crunched on the stalks. They enjoyed eating the leaves and stems, too!

So, they ate and ate, but they didn't do any exercise and became extremely fat. At the beginning of the fourth week, one panda started to try to walk again, but he was so fat that he couldn't run. He could only walk very slowly.

And, that's why pandas move so slowly!

Karissa Cheung studies in year 8 at Yew Chung International School. Her hobby is gymnastics. She has been learning for over six years. In her free time, she loves to read books.

Why Pandas Have Black Eye Patches

Kelvin Ko
To my best friend, Jeff

Many years ago, pandas didn't have black eye patches. They had round black ears and small dark brown eyes. Their faces were white.

One day, two pandas decided to play outside. First they played hide and seek. They played until they felt bored. Next, they played tag. They ran until they felt tired. Then they decided to play soccer. They had no soccer ball, so they tied up the bamboo in the shape of a ball. They played soccer for two weeks.

After all those games, they were exhausted so they sat down and chatted. The pandas told stories to each other. They didn't sleep for one whole month.

Finally, they were so tired that they went to sleep. They slept for seven days.

When they woke up, they had huge dark circles around their eyes.

That's why pandas have black eye patches.

Kelvin Ko
is going into form 2 in Raimondi College. His hobbies are tennis and badminton. He likes playing on the computer in his free time. He also likes traveling to other places with his mum and dad. His favorite trip was last Christmas when he went to Egypt.

BEFORE...

Why Pandas Like to Eat Bamboo

Valarie Lam
For my lovely family that shares
my love for others

Long, long ago, pandas did not eat bamboo. They ate lotus leaves.

One day villagers came with many children collecting lotus leaves. They saw children wrapping rice with lotus leaves. They could smell the fantastic fragrance. The pandas soon felt hungry. They could find no more lotus leaves.

The pandas went to the villagers' homes. They saw the villagers were gone. They only saw bits of lotus leaves. "Oh, no!" said a mother panda because her baby was crying. They wanted the lotus leaves back from the villagers because they felt hungry. They finished eating the bits of lotus leaves. They searched and tried to find something else to eat.

The mother panda had an idea, "Why don't we try eating bamboo?" So they tried it. First they ate the stems. They loved them. Next they ate the leaves. They thought the leaves tasted like another version of the lotus leaves. Then everyone, even the baby, loved the bamboo!

So from that day on till now pandas eat bamboo.

Valarie Lam
is going into grade 4 at Hong Kong International School. She loves multiplication and division. Her hobbies are reading and writing. Her favorite color is pink. Her favorite food is penne pasta with tuna and cheese.

Why Pandas Are Fat

Andrew Lau
To my sister, Alison

Many years ago, pandas were thin. They were the most popular animal in the bamboo forest. Everyone loved them.

One day the monkeys found a place which had a lot of bamboo! The pandas loved eating bamboo, so they wanted to go there to feed, but they didn't want to walk because they were so tired. They asked the monkeys to help them get the bamboo.

The monkeys brought the bamboo to the pandas and the pandas started crunching the tasty bamboo. The pandas asked the monkeys for more bamboo, but there weren't enough monkeys to carry all the bamboo that would feed the pandas. So the pandas asked the horses and lions to help get the bamboo. Day after day, the animals carried heavy loads of bamboo for the pandas. The pandas got no exercise so they were getting fatter.

One day the lions became very angry at the pandas.

Since the lions were the strongest, they needed to get the most bamboo and they had no time to rest. They shouted angrily at the pandas, "We are not helping you any more." The horses refused to carry the bamboo since the lions did not help. The monkeys were too old to carry the bamboo. The pandas had no bamboo to eat so they had to find bamboo by themselves.

The pandas asked the monkeys for the map giving directions to the bamboo forest. After one month, the pandas arrived at the forest. They saw a lot of beautiful plants. They ate and ate and ate. They never left this place. They did only a little exercise.

So, now all pandas are fat.

Andrew Lau
is in year 6 at Pun U Wah Yan Association Primary School. He is a Scout and he likes to go camping. He loves playing table tennis, basketball and computer games. He also loves reading! He reads one or two books a week.

1st...

2nd...

BLACK PAINT

Final

Why Pandas Have Eye Patches

Clare Leung
For The Leung Family and
my favorite author, Judy Blume

Clare Leung
studies in St. Paul's Convent School. She loves drawing and dancing. She likes cycling in Shatin with her family. Her passion is singing. Her favorite songs are "A Whole New World" and "Somewhere Over the Rainbow".

Once upon a time, pandas had no eye patches, but things changed.

There once was a very proud panda. He was very good at swimming but he was extremely proud about it. At first the other pandas adored him very much, but one day he said one sentence to make things different. He said,

"You all are not as talented as I! I am the best swimmer!"

Now that made his mates dislike him. So they decided to play a trick on him.

When the proud panda was swimming, the other pandas tiptoed into his changing room with a tin of black paint. They put black paint around the eye pieces of his goggles. Of course, the proud panda didn't know that.

The next day, he went swimming again. After practicing, he took off his goggles and saw himself in the mirror. The other pandas teased him about the eye patches. He felt embarrassed. He decided never to look down on others again.

And, that's why pandas have eye patches!

Why Pandas Have Black Eye Patches

Vicky Lim
To Judy Butler, who is crazy about pandas

Many years ago, panda's eye patches were muddy brown. It had black legs, black ears, a black chest and a black strip across its back. The rest of its body was white.

There was once a curious panda which lived in the bamboo forest high on a mountain in China. One afternoon, the panda strolled down the mountain to get to its favorite place for a snack. It saw a man doing something with a white sack, so it waited and waited until the man disappeared.

The panda crept closer and closer. It saw twenty-eight white sacks of black powder. The panda dipped its paw into the powder. It felt like dust, but it was black. The panda thought and thought until it had an idea. "Aha, I know what to do!" It grabbed some black dust and wiped it onto its muddy brown eye patches. Then the panda lumbered further down the mountain to the river. When it looked into the water, it saw its eye patches were now black.

"I can't believe it. My eye patches match my body color."

That night its mom said, "You had better wash that black powder off your face!"

"But, Mom, I like this color on my eye patches."

Mom handed little panda a face towel. It tried to wipe the black powder off its face. The powder wouldn't come off.

So, now all pandas have black eye patches.

Vicky Lim
is in year 8 at Kiangsu & Chekiang College, International Section. She loves playing with her friends. Her favorite sports are horseback riding and mountain biking. Her favorite movie is "Pirates of the Caribbean" (all three movies). Whenever she has free time, she talks to her friends on MSN or walks her cute schnauzer.

Why Pandas Have Black Eye Patches

Joanna Lo
For my little sister, Jackie

Long ago, pandas didn't have black eye patches. They had black ears, black legs, white tails and tiny brown eyes. But, pandas had no black eye patches.

One day a young panda was walking along a path eating bamboo. She suddenly saw a pot filled with something black. She stuck her head in and PLOP! Something hit her eyes. She walked down the mountain feeling weird.

All the other pandas saw that panda. They thought she was so pretty with her black eye patches. So all of the other pandas decided they wanted eye patches. They asked her where she got the eye patches.

She said, "What eye patches?"

Her friends said, "There is black stuff around your eyes."

"I think I heard a PLOP sound when I stuck my head in a gigantic pot on top of the hill." She walked to the closest river and looked in. She saw her black eye patches. She really liked them.

The other pandas said, "Let's go to the top of the hill." So they strolled up the hill. They saw the pot and one by one stuck their heads in. When they lifted their heads up, each panda had eye patches. When the ink plopped up it made all different shapes of eye patches.

After all the pandas got eye patches, the girl panda felt quite frustrated because the other pandas had copied her. At night she crept out of her tree house and went to the river with a bucket. She filled the bucket with water and carried it to the other pandas' tree houses. She poured the water on each of the pandas' faces, but the black stuff did not come off. She felt really angry because she wanted to be unique.

So, now all pandas have black eye patches!

Joanna Lo
goes to Chinese International School. She has just finished year 4. Her hobbies are drawing and reading. Her favorite color is purple. Her passion is ice skating. She loves learning new jumps and spins.

Why Pandas Have Short Black Legs

Joyce Lo

For Dad, Mum, brother Alex and
my best friend, Lilian

Many years ago, pandas had long white legs.

One day there was a very heavy rainstorm in the forest. The pandas were very frightened because it was the heaviest rainstorm they had ever seen. Therefore, they hid in their own caves to protect themselves.

However, the mother pandas gave birth to a lot of baby pandas. Sometimes the mothers gave birth to ten babies! They wanted to save more space to protect their babies so they wrapped their long legs with pieces of black cloth. **They bent the babies' legs and wrapped them very tightly.** Finally all of the baby pandas had enough space to stay in the caves. The storm lasted for a few years.

One day, the storm stopped. The mother pandas could finally take away the black cloth from their babies' legs. When they unwrapped the black cloth, they found that the babies' legs had become short and black. They discovered that the dye from the black cloth had made their fur change from white to black.

So now pandas have short black legs. And, the mother pandas only give birth to one or two panda babies.

Joyce Lo

was born in Hong Kong in 1994 and is now studying at St. Paul's Secondary School. Next year, she will go to Sherborne Girls' School in England. She likes reading, especially fiction. She loves playing computer games and surfing the net. She enjoys spending time with friends. She thinks pandas' movements are cute and funny.

1st...

2nd...

Final

Why Pandas Are Black and White

Sabrina Ma

For my English teacher, Judy Butler,
who loves pandas

A billion years ago, pandas were all white. One hot, shiny day, panda was putting on his white swimming trunks, about to go to the beach. Panda was having a beach party and he felt a little cold so he wore a tank top, earmuffs and knee socks. Everything he wore was black, except his white swimming trunks. He remembered his mom said to wear sunglasses when he went to the beach to protect his eyes. His sunglasses were black, too. He looked in the mirror and said, "Perfect!" Then he went off to the beach party.

After he came home, he took everything off and went to the mirror and said, "Ahhhhhh, what happened to me? I'm black and white." He had black on his legs, arms, chest, eyes and ears because everything black that he had worn had faded onto his fur! "How am I supposed to go out and meet my friends tonight?"

He tried to figure out how he could cover the black so everyone wouldn't laugh at him.

He would be very embarrassed if he couldn't cover the black. Then he thought of an idea. He would call his friends and say he was sick and couldn't go to the dinner. His friends said they would come and visit him, but he said he had to rest. So his friends didn't bother him.

He spent the next two weeks of his life at home because he didn't want people to make fun of his looks. After two weeks panda had no food left so he had to go to the shop and buy food. At first he didn't dare to, but then he was very hungry so he went down to the Pandan Shop. Then he saw a female who was single. So he talked to her and welcomed her to come to his house and have dinner. She was a beauty in his eyes. After they knew each other for a few weeks, they fell in love.

One day he wondered why the other pandas weren't laughing at him. Maybe the others didn't think he was funny at all. When he met the girl panda the next time, panda said he wanted to marry her and she agreed. They had a lot of babies. All the babies had black tank tops, black earmuffs, black knee socks and black sunglasses like their dad.

From then on, all pandas were black and white.

Sabrina Ma

goes to Chinese International School in Hong Kong. She likes to read books, especially crime scene mysteries. She loves to write; she has already written twenty-five stories. She likes to play the piano, especially "My Heart Will Go On" from the movie "Titanic".

Why Pandas Eat Bamboo

Carissa Ng
To my family and my best friend, Sally

A long, long time ago, pandas were very fat because of eating too much sugar. All the rivers that ran through their habitat contained syrup. The pandas drank a lot of the river water, which made them fat. The other animals also drank the river water, but they never grew fat because they knew how to control their quantity of liquid.

The flowers in their region were very delicious because they contained a lot of sugar. These were the pandas' favorites. They could not resist them. They loved them so much that they never got tired of eating them. All those sweet flowers made them gain more weight. The pandas were so fat that the only animals that could serve them were the squirrels as they were the strongest of the little animals.

Twenty years passed and the pandas were as big as Mount Everest. The squirrels got sick and tired of climbing up the giant pandas to feed them and called a meeting of all the animals. The smartest animal, the giraffe, was in charge.

"The pandas are too obese; we have to do something," King Giraffe said.

"I think we should kill them!" King Lion shouted.

The giraffes frowned, "No, we do not want pandas to be extinct."

"I think we should not let them eat. I mean, we serve them so we can control them in a way, right?" King Squirrel asked.

"You want to kill them as well? No. We cannot do that. Are there any other ideas?" questioned King Giraffe.

"I've got the greatest idea!" King Hedgehog said.

"What is it?" the giraffes inquired.

"There are so many plants in this world. Why don't we go on a hunt to discover the plant which doesn't contain any sugar?" King Hedgehog said proudly.

The giraffes smiled, "Why didn't you suggest this earlier?"

"Save the best for last!" King Hedgehog winked.

It took over three years to find the right kind of plant. During those years they occasionally gathered together to discuss the newest discovery, yet none of them was right for the pandas. Finally they found the right plant. They named it bamboo. It contained juice and nutrients, everything that pandas need.

The pandas ate and ate the bamboo. They didn't care what it was, as long as it was yummy. After ten years, the pandas were chubby, but not humongous anymore. From that day on, they never stopped eating bamboo.

And, that's why pandas eat bamboo.

Carissa Ng
is thirteen. She attends South Island School and is studying in year 9. She is interested in fashion and loves to design clothes in her free time. She also enjoys swimming and loves yummy food.

Why Pandas Eat Bamboo

Long Hei Ng
For Mom and Dad

Long, long ago, pandas didn't eat bamboo. They ate little mushrooms and grass. They wanted to eat French fries with ketchup.

One night panda woke up. There was a bright light in front of him. It was the panda fairy. Panda said, "I want to eat French fries with ketchup. I looked at a cookbook and I read about French fries and they looked delicious."

The fairy said, "Well, in China there is no ketchup and there are no French fries, but you can eat bamboo because there are a lot of bamboo plants in China."

"Ai yah! I don't know what bamboo is?"

The fairy said, "I will let you taste it." She brought some dark green bamboo to him.

The panda ate it. "Hey! It is delicious!"

The fairy said, "It is because it is the dark green one."

And that's why pandas eat bamboo. They forgot about the French fries.

And they love bamboo now!

Long Hei Ng
goes to St. James' Settlement Kindergarten. He likes the color bronze. He likes to play with Lego and do experiments with water. He likes to go on vacations.

Why Pandas Have Black Eye Patches

William Scown
Dedicated to Caroline Scown

Long, long ago, pandas didn't have eye patches.

One day, the panda went to sleep under a tree. Then a snow leopard came. It punched the panda in the left eye. Then it punched the panda in the right eye. Then the leopard raced away.

The panda felt the punches and he woke up. He felt pain! Then he went to a nearby river. He looked into the water. His reflection looked all mixed up. He saw black eye patches. He knew that when the leopard punched him his eyes turned black.

The next day the leopard punched him in the eyes again. The day after that, the leopard knocked the panda in the eyes again. Year after year after year the leopard socked the panda in the eyes.

And that's why pandas have black eye patches.

William Scown
goes to Hong Kong
International School. He
is studying kung fu for his
black belt. He loves to eat
dim sum and pizza.
He loves math and art.
He enjoys playing light
sabers with his friends.
He also likes to catch
insects and geckos.

Why Pandas Have Short Tails

Marco Tao
For my teacher Mrs. Gooding
and her new baby

Many years ago, pandas had two meter long tails. Their tails were white and fluffy.

One time, a panda named Lam Lam climbed on top of a cave. He didn't know that snow leopards lived there. When the panda walked on top of the cave, his long tail was dangling in front of the mouth of the cave. The leopard saw it. He thought, "Heh, heh! My bed is so hard. I'm going to use that long tail to make a comfortable pillow for sleeping."

So, the snow leopard used his front paw to snatch the long tail. He curled it round and round and round. It made a soft cushion that he could relax his head on.

Lam Lam was shocked. "Where's my tail? Oh my goodness! My tail is only eighteen centimeters long!"

So, that's why pandas now have short tails.

Marco Tao
is beginning year 5 at Chinese International School. He likes to play Monopoly with his parents when he has free time. His favorite sport is tennis; he also likes swimming and rugby. He likes ice cream, pizza, s'mores and buckaroos.

NOW

BEFORE...

Why Pandas Are Black and White

Taryn Wan
For my mom

Many, many years ago, pandas were white. Their bodies, legs, ears, faces and even their noses were white. They lived in the bamboo forest in China.

One day an artist living in a village near the bamboo forest decided to take his ink and brushes and paper and walk up the mountain to find pandas. He wanted to draw pictures of pandas eating bamboo.

He found a rock to sit on. First he sketched the bamboo on a piece of paper. After that he sketched the pandas eating bamboo. The artist accidentally knocked over a bucket of ink that was next to him.

Two pandas were chasing each other. Neither of the pandas saw the ink that was right in front of them, so they slipped. Their faces and legs were black. They rolled over and now their backs were black. The artist tried to help them wipe off the ink, but it wouldn't come off.

So, now all pandas are black and white.

Taryn Wan
is going to year 5 at Hong Kong International School. She likes shopping for DVDs and shoes. She likes to play badminton and four square. She loves swimming with her friend and playing with her friend's dog. Her favorite color is green.

Why Pandas Are Fat and Lazy

Talia Yim
To Judy Allen because she likes pandas, too

Long ago, pandas were slim animals and they were hardworking. Every morning at eight o'clock, pandas had to wake up and search for food.

But one day, there was a huge snowstorm. All the pandas stayed in their homes. It snowed and snowed so the pandas had no food left.

A year later, the snowstorm stopped but when the pandas went out of their houses, all the bamboo was gone. The bamboo was under the heavy snow, but the pandas could not get it.

The other countries heard of the big snowstorm and they delivered much bamboo to the pandas. The pandas ate it quickly and they didn't search for food any more. They ate a lot of bamboo and became fatter and fatter.

In China, many people thought pandas were cute so they wanted to protect the pandas in their country, and they gave homes to the pandas and provided bamboo for them to eat. The pandas were very safe there. They slept and ate every day. Now they were too lazy to search for food.

So now, all pandas are fat and lazy.

Talia Yim
is a student of St. Paul's Primary Catholic School. She enjoys dancing and reading. She likes watching television and playing computer games in her free time. Her favorite color is green and her favorite food is abalone, although it's very expensive.

THE GOLDEN PHOENIX

Why Pandas Are Huge

Alyssa Yoon
To all the pandas in the world

Long, long ago when humans were not on earth, pandas were tiny. They were as tiny as guinea pigs. They had some huge problems. The pandas always got stepped on. They could only eat grass. They didn't get noticed. They really wished that they would be immense.

In the bamboo forest lived a magical golden phoenix. The phoenix could grant wishes. One day when the pandas were eating grass near a spring, the phoenix was taking his exercise, making a blaze of color in the sky. He got very thirsty and went in search of water. The amazing creature spied a spring. He swooped down to get a drink of water. While he was quenching his thirst, he overheard the pandas talking about how they wished to be bigger.

"You wish to be huge, so you shall be huge," boomed the voice of the phoenix. Suddenly there was a cloud surrounding the pandas. The cloud disappeared with a loud KA-BOOM! Right then the pandas became bigger than guinea pigs! They were bigger than the biggest wart hogs! They were huge. They were so happy! Now they would not get stepped on! When the other animals saw the pandas, they almost fainted because they were so amazed at their new size.

The pandas threw a party celebrating not having to eat the plain grass. Instead they could eat the wondrous bamboo! They invited the golden monkeys, the red pandas, the fleecy white sheep, and the snorting wart hogs. And, the guest of honor was the mystic golden phoenix! Everything they ate came from the bamboo.

And that's why pandas are huge!

Alyssa Yoon
is a 4th grader at Hong Kong International School. Her passion is reading and her favorite genre of books is historical fiction. She also likes drawing. Her three favorite subjects are reading, writing and social studies. Her favorite sport is tennis.

Why Pandas Have Eye Patches

Lauren Yoon
To my best friend, Vivian

Lauren Yoon
is seven years old and is in grade 2 at Hong Kong International School.

Her favorite thing to do is reading. She loves to play tennis. Her favorite animal is the horse. She loves to ride them.

Long, long ago all pandas had white faces. They had no eye patches. They had tiny dark brown eyes and small black noses and round black ears.

One morning two pandas were playing in the bamboo forest. They were sisters. They saw a pot of black liquid beside a short bamboo tree. There was a small brush next to the pot. One of the pandas put its paw into the ink. She lifted her paw and showed the other panda. The other panda did the same. One panda picked up the paintbrush and dipped it into the ink. She put the black around her eyes like circles. And the other panda did the same.

They went home to their small cave. Their mother saw their eyes with the black circles.

"What have you done to your faces?"

"We found some black liquid in a pot and we put it around our eyes."

"Let's go to the lake now! You girls must wash that black liquid off!" They all walked to the lake. Their mother tried to wash it off. She couldn't!

And that's why all pandas have eye patches.

Amazing Facts about Pandas

Claire Doole/WWF-Canon

- Wild pandas are only found in the mountain ranges of southwestern China.

- There are around 1,600 pandas in the wild.

- Female pandas can only give birth once a year to 1-2 babies. A baby panda only weighs about 100 grams.

- A panda's average life span is 20-25 years in the wild and up to 30 years in captivity.

- An adult panda can weigh about 100-150 kg and grow up to 150 cm long.

- Pandas are classified as bears and have the digestive system of a carnivore, but they have adapted to a vegetarian diet of bamboo.

- Pandas spend about 14 hours a day eating.

- A panda may eat 12-38 kg of bamboo a day.

- A panda's back molars are seven times bigger than a human's molars so that it can crush the bamboo.

- Pandas have a wrist bone that can move like a thumb so they are able to grasp the bamboo and eat while sitting up.